A Home for the Sock Monkeys

**Written by
Tina Payne Sarafa and
Karen Silber Miller**

ISBN: 1451565070
ISBN-13: 9781451565072
LCCN: 2010904250
CreateSpace, North Charleston, South Carolina

Tina dedicates this book to her three boys
(Matthew, Johnny and Nicky).
A special thanks goes out to her sister Tammy,
all of our monkeys, and the stories we shared.

Karen dedicates this book to her son, Daniel.

In a cozy little house many years ago,

Granny Cox decided that she would sew

Cuddly toy monkeys using men's brown socks,

And cotton, paint, and buttons she had in a box.

Each monkey was soft with a button nose,

And big bright lips as red as a rose.

They had long skinny tails that you could twirl,

They could be playful friends for any boy or girl.

Granny's children were grown and lived far away,

So she decided in her house the monkeys would stay,

They were a happy family, and she gave them
all names.

They talked for hours and played fun, silly games.

Lullabell was sweet, happy, wise, and smart,

She taught the others right from wrong from the start,

One day Granny put her in the washing machine,

Because she fell into dirt and needed to get clean.

Lullabell got clean but her face became quite pale,

The other monkeys thought she would cry and wail,

But she said, "How I look does not matter to me,

As long as I am part of this happy family."

Wendy liked to dress in clothes with ribbons and lace.

She was glad Granny gave her such a pretty face,

But she was mad that Granny did not give her a tail.

She said, "This is so much worse than being too pale."

Wendy was bossy and made herself the Monkey Queen.

When she didn't get her way, she was very, very mean.

She told the other monkeys, "If you don't do what I say,

Then I'll tell Granny Cox she must send you away."

Wendy was also tricky and would say to the others,

"It would be an honor my sisters and brothers,

To give up your tail for your Monkey Queen,

It is better that your tails on me to be seen."

Wendy tried every trick and offer she could,

To make the other monkeys give up their tails for good,

"If you give me your tail I'll like you the best,"

Was one of the promises she gave to the rest.

Wendy knew it was wrong for her to steal,

Which is why she wanted to make a deal.

If the monkeys gave her a tail it wouldn't be wrong,

But the other monkeys would not go along.

Lullabell said, "You are fine the way you are,

You don't need a tail, you will still go far,

You are pretty and funny and we all love you so,

You are a special monkey, I want you to know."

Henry was the smartest monkey of them all.

He had a cone-shaped head and was very, very tall.

He helped the others with homework and told them to study.

Henry was so friendly, he was everyone's buddy.

Timothy was sweet, but also quite shy.

He didn't like to talk too much and no one knew just why.

He did everything that Wendy wanted each and every day.

The only thing he would not do is give his tail away.

There were fifteen monkeys in the home of
Granny Cox,

Fifteen soft, cuddly monkeys made from men's
brown socks.

They were happy little monkeys until that one sad day,

When Granny told them it was time she had to
move away.

"I am getting very old and so the time has come,

To leave this cozy little house and live with my son,

My room is very small so you cannot come along,

You must all stick together and try to be strong."

She took them to the toy store owned by kind Mr. Fox,

And asked him to find a new home for her monkeys made of socks.

She said they were a family and together must be sold.

He said that would be hard because they were homemade and old.

With his fancy new dolls and shiny new cars, he was afraid

That no one would choose monkeys that were not newly made.

He said, "Why would children turn down a brand new box,

To buy a bunch of monkeys, made from old brown socks?"

Wendy was most afraid that Mr. Fox was right.

"We're going to be in the toy store forever and
a night.

No one wants a monkey who does not have a tail,

No one wants a monkey whose face is old and pale."

"Who will want a monkey who is so very shy?

Who will want a monkey who is taller than the sky?

Each of us is different, and even with a queen,

How can we be chosen over toys so new and clean?"

"Don't worry," Granny told them. "You were made with special care.

Even though you're different, you still have love to share.

These new toys may be shiny, and have a fancy box,

But they are not made by hand, like you monkeys made of socks."

The next day in walked two little girls.

They were sisters with pretty, long, shiny curls.

They said, "Look at that monkey without a tail,

Look at that monkey whose face is so pale!"

"There are fifteen fine monkeys here," said Mr. Fox.

"They are part of a family, these monkeys made
of socks."

"Oh, Mother, can we buy them?" the girls yelled
and yelled.

"These monkeys look so lonely, they need to be held."

"They are not new," said the mother, "and there are fifteen."

"But we can't break up a family, that would be mean!"

The girls promised to love them and play with them each day,

If these soft, cuddly monkeys could go home with them to stay.

"Granny was right," all the happy monkeys thought.

They would miss Granny, but they were glad to be bought.

Wendy felt better about having no tail,

And Lullabell, as always, was proud of being pale.

Timothy hoped the little girls would help him not be shy.

He knew they were so sweet, it would be easy to try.

Henry hoped the little girls had books for him to read,

He planned to be a doctor, to help monkeys in need.

The little girls placed them in a box with great care.

They couldn't wait to bring them to the new home they would share.

The monkeys were happy as they rode in the box.

There was a new home for the monkeys made of socks.

Made in the USA
Las Vegas, NV
06 November 2022

58941015R00024